# » RETURN OF THE
# FIRST AVENGER

Written by
**Michael Siglain**

Based on Marvel's *The Avengers*
Motion Picture Written by
**Joss Whedon**

Illustrated by
**Lee Garbett, John Lucas,**
and
**Lee Duhig**

Based on
Marvel Comics' *The Avengers*

MARVEL
NEW YORK

www.marvel.com

TM & © 2012 Marvel & Subs.

Printed in the United States of America
First Edition
1 3 5 7 9 10 8 6 4 2
G658-7729-4-12032
ISBN 978-1-4231-5482-2

This is the story of the

return of the First Avenger.

Steve Rogers wasn't always

a Super Hero.

And he wasn't always

known as

Captain America.

Steve took part in a very

special army experiment

called Project: Rebirth.

It turned Steve from

sick and thin

to big and strong.

Steve Rogers became

America's first Super-Soldier.

He was now known

as Captain America,

the First Avenger!

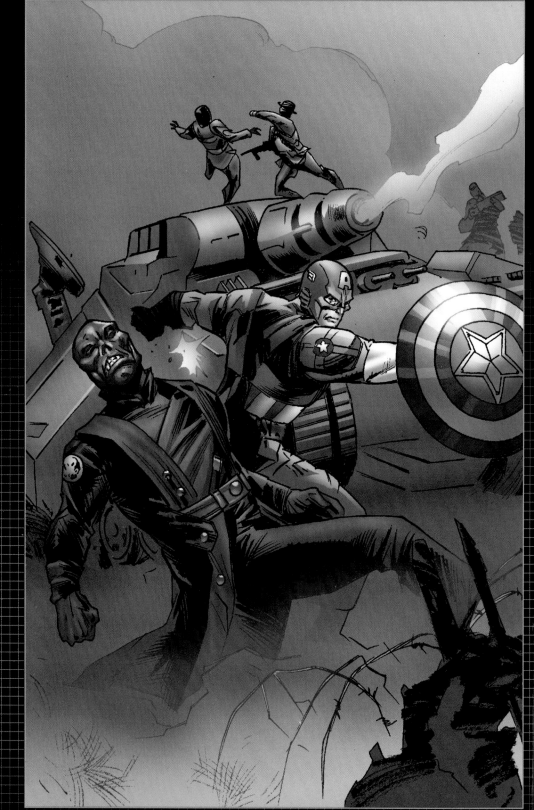

Captain America

fought for justice with

the Howling Commandos

against the evil Red Skull

and his HYDRA army!

During World War II,

Captain America

was lost in the Arctic

while saving the world.

He stopped a plane

full of bombs.

Captain America

and the plane he was flying

sank under the cold ice.

Captain America was trapped

inside the plane and frozen in

the Arctic for many, many years.

Decades passed, until finally
Nick Fury's S.H.I.E.L.D. team
found Cap and the plane.
S.H.I.E.L.D.'s plan was to bring
Captain America back to life!

Steve Rogers awoke

almost seventy years later.

He was very confused.

Steve didn't know where

he was, but he knew he

had to escape!

Steve ran into the middle of
Times Square in New York City.
There, he met Nick Fury,
the director of S.H.I.E.L.D.
Fury explained what had
happened to Steve and that he
was there to help.

Steve spent a lot of time

watching news footage

to learn what had happened

while he was frozen.

It seemed to him that the world

still needed a Super-Soldier.

Steve exercised to keep
his mind and body strong.
And when Nick Fury asked
Steve to join a very special
team of Super Heroes,
Steve said yes.
The First Avenger
had returned!

Nick Fury introduced Steve
to his new teammates. He met
Tony Stark, who is Iron Man;
Clint Barton, who is Hawkeye;
Natasha Romanoff, who is Black
Widow; the mighty Thor; and
scientist Dr. Bruce Banner.

But Steve couldn't go into battle

without a new uniform.

He was given a new suit,

and soon Captain America

was ready for action!

It wasn't long before a
Super Villain threatened the
safety of the world.
Captain America and his
teammates fought against
Loki, Thor's evil brother
from Asgard.

After Bruce Banner changed
into the incredible Hulk,
the heroes were finally assembled.
Steve Rogers was happy to be
fighting for freedom and justice
as a member of the Avengers!